THE POPULARITY OF MEDITATION & SPIRITUAL PRACTICES

Seeking Inner Peace

RELIGION & MODERN CULTURE
Title List

THE POPULARITY OF MEDITATION
& SPIRITUAL PRACTICES
Seeking Inner Peace

by Kenneth McIntosh, M.Div.,
and Marsha McIntosh

Mason Crest Publishers
Philadelphia

Mason Crest Publishers Inc.
370 Reed Road
Broomall, Pennsylvania 19008
(866) MCP-BOOK (toll free)

First printing
1 2 3 4 5 6 7 8 9 10

Library of Congress Cataloging-in-Publication Data

McIntosh, Kenneth, 1959–
  The popularity of meditation & spiritual practices : seeking inner peace / by Kenneth McIntosh and Marsha McIntosh.
      p. cm. — (Religion and modern culture)
  Includes bibliographical references and index.
  ISBN 1-59084-980-9 (alk. paper)   1-59084-970-1 (series)
  1. Meditation—Juvenile literature. 2. Spiritual life—Juvenile literature. I. Title: Popularity of meditation and spiritual practices. II. McIntosh, Marsha. III. Title. IV. Series.
  BL627.M3955 2006
  204'.3—dc22
                          2005011453

Produced by Harding House Publishing Service, Inc.
www.hardinghousepages.com
Interior design by Dianne Hodack.
Cover design by MK Bassett-Harvey.
Printed in India.

CONTENTS

INTRODUCTION

by Dr. Marcus J. Borg

You are about to begin an important and exciting experience: the study of modern religion. Knowing about religion—and religions—is vital for understanding our neighbors, whether they live down the street or across the globe.

Despite the modern trend toward religious doubt, most of the world's population continues to be religious. Of the approximately six billion people alive today, around two billion are Christians, one billion are Muslims, 800 million are Hindus, and 400 million are Buddhists. Smaller numbers are Sikhs, Shinto, Confucian, Taoist, Jewish, and indigenous religions.

Religion plays an especially important role in North America. The United States is the most religious country in the Western world: about 80 percent of Americans say that religion is "important" or "very important" to them. Around 95 percent say they believe in God. These figures are very different in Europe, where the percentages are much smaller. Canada is "in between": the figures are lower than for the United States, but significantly higher than in Europe. In Canada, 68 percent of citizens say religion is of "high importance," and 81 percent believe in God or a higher being.

The United States is largely Christian. Around 80 percent describe themselves as Christian. In Canada, professing Christians are 77 percent of the population. But religious diversity is growing. According to Harvard scholar Diana Eck's recent book *A New Religious America*, the United States has recently become the most religiously diverse country in the world. Canada is also a country of great religious variety.

Fifty years ago, religious diversity in the United States meant Protestants, Catholics, and Jews, but since the 1960s, immigration from Asia, the Middle East, and Africa has dramatically increased the number of people practicing other religions. There are now about six million Muslims, four million Buddhists, and a million Hindus in the United States. To compare these figures to two historically important Protestant denominations in the United States, about 3.5 million are Presbyterians and 2.5 million are Episcopalians. There are more Buddhists in the United States than either of these denominations, and as many Muslims as the two denominations combined. This means that knowing about other religions is not just knowing about people in other parts of the world—but about knowing people in our schools, workplaces, and neighborhoods.

Moreover, religious diversity does not simply exist between religions. It is found within Christianity itself:

• There are many different forms of Christian worship. They range from Quaker silence to contemporary worship with rock music to traditional liturgical worship among Catholics and Episcopalians to Pentecostal enthusiasm and speaking in tongues.

- Christians are divided about the importance of an afterlife. For some, the next life—a paradise beyond death—is their primary motive for being Christian. For other Christians, the afterlife does not matter nearly as much. Instead, a relationship with God that transforms our lives this side of death is the primary motive.
- Christians are divided about the Bible. Some are biblical literalists who believe that the Bible is to be interpreted literally and factually as the inerrant revelation of God, true in every respect and true for all time. Other Christians understand the Bible more symbolically as the witness of two ancient communities—biblical Israel and early Christianity—to their life with God.

Christians are also divided about the role of religion in public life. Some understand "separation of church and state" to mean "separation of religion and politics." Other Christians seek to bring Christian values into public life. Some (commonly called "the Christian Right") are concerned with public policy issues such as abortion, prayer in schools, marriage as only heterosexual, and pornography. Still other Christians name the central public policy issues as American imperialism, war, economic injustice, racism, health care, and so forth. For the first group, values are primarily concerned with individual behavior. For the second group, values are also concerned with group behavior and social systems. The study of religion in North America involves not only becoming aware of other religions but also becoming aware of differences within Christianity itself. Such study can help us to understand people with different convictions and practices.

And there is one more reason why such study is important and exciting: religions deal with the largest questions of life. These questions are intellectual, moral, and personal. Most centrally, they are:

- What is real? The religions of the world agree that "the real" is more than the space-time world of matter and energy.
- How then shall we live?
- How can we be "in touch" with "the real"? How can we connect with it and become more deeply centered in it?

This series will put you in touch with other ways of seeing reality and how to live.

Chapter 1

SEEKING INNER PEACE

RELIGION & MODERN CULTURE

Soren Gordhamer teaches teenagers—but he does not teach English, math, or science. The classrooms in which he teaches are somewhat unusual as well. To reach his students, Gordhamer must walk through a series of checkpoints and automatically locked doors. As he walks down a hall, one of the students greets him.

"Yoga-man."

Gordhamer recognizes the student, a young man named Chris. Gordhamer has not been asked to visit Chris's class today, but the young man is insistent. They walk into a classroom with eight kids and no teacher. Chris gets the other students' attention. "Yo, check this out. We're going to do a meditation. Everybody chill and listen to him."

Soren asks the students to close their eyes for meditation. Chris interrupts. "They gotta sit up straight first." He shows them how to do that. Soren Gordhamer leads the class in a short meditation and ends just as their regular teacher returns to the classroom. She sees her class sitting in a circle looking very calm, and she is pleased.

Gordhamer teaches meditation for teens incarcerated in the Bronx, Queens, and Harlem, New York. He tells about his experiences in the book *Blue Jean Buddha.* Why does he work in such a difficult environment? Gordhamer recalls his own teenage years when he was, as he puts it, a "bored, confused and suffering" teen. Meditating helped him gain self-confidence and a sense of peace.

MILLIONS MEDITATE

In the 1960s, when the Yoga Maharishi Mahesh Yogi introduced Transcendental Meditation (TM) to North America, meditation was something that only "hippies" and other **nonconformists** did. A few decades later, meditation was becoming more common—but "ordinary" people still assumed it was for "New Agers" and Californians. In the twenty-first century, however, meditation and similar spiritual techniques enjoy widespread popularity. Young and old people of all different religions and careers practice meditation, yoga, and other spiritual disciplines for a broad variety of reasons.

According to *Time* magazine writer Joel Stein, in his August 2003 article titled "Just Say Om," "Ten million American adults now say they practice some form of meditation regularly, twice as many as a decade ago." In fact, says Stein:

It's becoming increasingly hard to avoid meditation. It is offered in schools, hospitals, law firms, government buildings, corporate offices and prisons. There are specially marked meditation rooms

holistically: Done in a manner that involves all of something, especially the body.

nonconformists: People who do not act in expected ways or in accordance with current customs.

in airports alongside the prayer chapels and Internet kiosks. Meditation was the subject of a course at West Point, the spring 2002 issue of the *Harvard Law Review* and a few too many locker-room speeches by Lakers coach Phil Jackson.

There's even a high school in Fairfield, Iowa, where meditation is a vital part of every class. At the Maharishi School of the Age of Enlightenment (MSAE), students, faculty, and staff practice the TM technique together every day as part of their daily routine. MSAE has an impressive academic record: more than 95 percent of its graduates have been accepted at four-year colleges. Classes in grades nine through twelve consistently score in the top percentile on standardized tests such as the Iowa Tests of Educational Development. In addition, during the past five years, the school has produced more than ten times the national average of National Merit Scholar finalists.

In Canada, a 2001 mental health survey found that one in five Canadians said "meditation or relaxation" was a favored way to combat stress. Canada is home to a number of spiritual retreat centers that teach meditation. One of the best known is Gampo Abbey, focusing on Tibetan Buddhism, located in Pleasant Bay, Nova Scotia, and home to Buddhist monks and nuns. The Yoga Spa Ayurveda Centre in the Northumberland Hills in Brighton, Ontario, offers spa treatments based on Ayurveda, the ancient Indian art of health and healing.

At the same time, however, spiritual practices in general are less popular in Canada than in the United States. Taylor Nelson Sofres Intersearch (TNSI) conducted a comparison study of Canadian and U.S. citizens in 1999 and found that 87 percent of U.S. citizens say they "regularly engage in prayer or meditation," compared with 69 percent of Canadians.

THE NEW HOLISTIC VIEW OF HEALTH

Thousands of years ago, the ancient Greeks coined the phrase, "healthy mind, and healthy body." In the United States and Canada, it is only in the past several decades that scientists, doctors, business managers, social workers, and educators have realized the importance of treating people *holistically*. Leaders in a variety of professions have also realized that techniques traditionally associated with Eastern religion, such as meditation and yoga, have a broad range of benefits for body, mind, and spirit.

A major risk to health—both physical and emotional—is stress. Most people in the twenty-first century have way too much stress, and that causes high blood pressure, inability to think clearly, headaches, and general grouchiness. In an article on About.com, Barbara Bizou, a teacher of relaxation techniques, says:

Stress-related disorders are on the rise due to our complex and constantly changing world and we are seeing symptoms of fear

13

RELIGION & MODERN CULTURE

"Health, a light body, freedom from cravings, a glowing skin, sonorous voice, and fragrance of body: these signs indicate progress in the practice of meditation."

—*from the* Shvetashvatra Upanishad

and anxiety that have skyrocketed in the past decade. These directly impact our quality of life and our health.

An effective remedy for stress is meditation. "Meditation helps us to take a break from chaos," says Bizou.

As we move away from the stimuli of the moment, we are able to gain more clarity, focus and peace of mind. The key to meditation is it allows us to calm our fears and move into the present moment, and in that moment we can tap into a sense of peace— rather than worrying about the past or obsessing about the future.

Researchers also claim meditation may directly aid the human body's defense systems. Dr. Dean Ornish, for example, has done experiments that suggest meditation helps fight prostate cancer. The studies of Dr. Jon Kabat-Zinn at the University of Massachusetts have shown that meditation increases the strength of the body's immune system. Yet another medical study suggests meditation may also reduce the chances of women getting breast cancer. A Canadian study also found that meditation may help patients to overcome cancer.

Not only does meditation improve physical health, it may actually enable people to change from destructive to positive behaviors. A study at the Kings County North Rehabilitation Facility, a jail near Seattle, Washington, asked prisoners to practice Vipassana meditation for ten days, eleven hours a day. Only 56 percent of prisoners who meditated returned to jail within two years of their release, compared with a 75 percent return rate for prisoners who did not meditate. The former prisoners who meditated also used fewer drugs, drank less, and experienced less depression.

PART OF THE BIG PICTURE

Meditation and similar spiritual practices fit well with North American trends at the start of the twenty-first century. Americans and Canadians value health more than previous generations. The generation known as "baby boomers"—born between 1946 and 1964—are increasingly concerned about their health as they age. The boomers were also the generation that welcomed new forms of spirituality in the 1960s.

In 2002, Peter Emberley, a professor of political science and philosophy at Carleton University, set out to document the spiritual lives of Canadian baby boomers. Emberley noted that despite Canadians' reputation for spiritual disinterest, there were a small but highly influential number of baby boomers in Canada involved in nontraditional, nature-centered, or Eastern religious practices. This included several hundred wealthy Canadian citizens who retreat to the Himalayas for spiritual teaching.

In the United States, citizens are very involved with spiritual life. In spite of numerous technological advances in society, U.S. citizens are as devoted to religious and spiritual pursuits as ever in their history. At the same time, they are more religiously diverse. In the past, citizens sometimes referred to America as a "Judeo-Christian" nation. As many Muslims as Presbyterians live in America today, as well as millions of Hindus, Buddhists, and followers of other religions. While studies show that there is not as much interest in religion in Canada in general, religious diversity has increased there as well, along with an openness to new forms of spirituality.

"Meditation is not a way of making your mind quiet. It's a way of entering into the quiet that's already there—buried under the 50,000 thoughts the average person thinks every day."

—Deepak Chopra

MEDITATION MODELS

Meditation has become more popular in part because of prominent figures who follow the practice. Goldie Hawn, Shania Twain, Heather Graham, Richard Gere, and Al Gore all meditate. Actress Heather Graham says, "It's easy to spend a lot of time worrying and obsessing, but meditation puts me in a blissful place. At the end of the day, all that star stuff doesn't mean anything." Graham meditates daily for twenty minutes when she wakes up and twenty more in the afternoon. Former vice president Al Gore says of himself and his wife, Tipper, "We both believe in regular prayer, and we often pray together. But meditation—as distinguished from prayer—I highly recommend it."

Meditation and other spiritual exercises can be a vital part of religious belief, or an optional part of religious practice, or irrelevant to religious faith. In Buddhism, for example, meditation is a necessary part of religious practice. Meditation opens the way to awakening, one of the major goals of that religion. Meanwhile, in Christianity, Islam, and Judaism, prayer is a vital part of religion, while meditation is not required. In Christianity, salvation comes from Christ rather than any achievement in spiritual practices. Muslims must pray five times daily, but meditation is optional. In Judaism, morality and devotion to God are more important than specific spiritual exercises. Increasingly, people combine spiritual approaches, practicing Eastern religious forms alongside elements of Western religions. Still other practitioners regard meditation, yoga, and other exercises as primarily psychological—rather than religious—in nature.

Chapter 2

THE ROOTS OF MEDITATION

RELIGION & MODERN CULTURE

Who was the first man—or the first woman—to meditate? If you were to catch a glimpse of the original performers of meditation, you would probably see our earliest ancestors gazing in awe at the stars in the sky, or waiting for hours in the brush for a deer to come by them. Their lives were more connected to nature, and they probably had more time for the spiritual realm. According to Stephan Bodian, author of *Meditation for Dummies*, archaeologists have found cave paintings that date as far back as 15,000 years showing figures lying on the ground in a meditative posture. Scholars believe these to be **shamans** in a trance, asking the spirits for their blessing on the group's hunt.

Shamans, both male and female, used meditative trances to enter altered states of consciousness. When they were in these trances, they traveled to the "world of the spirits" and brought back spirit blessings, sacred wisdom, magical powers, and healing abilities to the tribe.

INDIAN ROOTS

For more than five thousand years, *sadhus* (wandering holy people) and *yogis* have practiced meditation in India. Although the Vedas, the earliest Indian scriptures, have no word for meditation, Vedic priests performed complicated rites that took much concentration. These rites turned into a type of prayerful meditation that included a devotional focus on a deity as well as use of breath control. India's best-known meditative traditions—yoga, tantra, and Buddhism—are founded on the Vedas.

Indian classical yoga teaches its students to withdraw from everyday life and merge with the reality of consciousness. The material world is thought to be an illusion. Students prepare themselves through *asanas*, or poses, then cultivate energy states through breathing techniques. They focus on repetition of a meaningful sound—a mantra. Ultimately, the person arrives at a state known as *samadhi*, a union with consciousness.

BUDDHIST MEDITATION

Buddha was a sixth-century BCE prince who, according to history, gave up his royal life to seek important answers to existence: why is there suffering, old age, and death? After trying a life of **asceticism** and yoga for many years, he rejected such an austere existence. He sat down

GLOSSARY

asceticism: Austerity and self-denial, especially as a way of life.

indigenous: Native to the area.

mysticism: The belief that personal communication with the Divine is achieved through intuition, faith, ecstasy, or sudden insight rather than through rational thought.

shamans: People who act as go-betweens for the physical and spiritual worlds, and who are said to have particular powers such as prophecy and healing.

Western: Found in or typical of countries, especially in Europe and North and South America, whose cultures and societies are influenced by Greek and Roman culture and Christianity.

yogis: People who study under a guru or other spiritual teacher of the Hindu religion.

under a tree and looked deeply into his own mind. Stephan Bodian writes, "After seven days and nights of deep meditation, he awoke to the nature of existence—and so the name Buddha, or 'the awakened one.'" The Buddha taught mindfulness, a type of meditation that enabled people to pay attention to their experiences from moment to moment. He taught that we suffer mainly because of two wrong beliefs: One, material things can be relied on for happiness and are permanent. Two, we have a permanent self that lives separately from other beings. He taught that everything in the world changes constantly, including our minds, emotions, and selves.

Before Buddhism left India at the end of the first millennium CE, it went through important changes. One branch, Theravada, emphasized a growing path to freedom mostly for priests and nuns. Another branch, called the Mahayana, offered the possibility of enlightenment to everyone. The Mahayana preached the ideal of the Bodhisattva—the person who dedicates her life to liberating others. From India, scholars brought Mahayana Buddhism over the Himalayas (the roof of the world) to China and Tibet. Here it mingled with spiritual teachings of the area and evolved into different traditions. One of them was Zen or Vajrayana Buddhism.

Zen was different from other forms of Buddhism, which focused largely on study of the scriptures. Through meditation, a Zen student was supposed to let go of attachments to the material world and put on more of the Buddha nature—the wisdom that is within each one of us. Zen introduced riddles called koans. These riddles seemed to be without answers but by meditation and intuition, a student could come up with the answers. An example of a koan is: "What was your original face before your parents were born?"

When Buddhism reached Tibet in the seventh century CE, it mixed with the *indigenous* religion called Bonpo. Tibetan Buddhists believed that the historical Buddha kept his most advanced teachings secret for centuries and then revealed them to Tibet as the Vajrayana ("the diamond way"). Instead of denying negative emotions, the Vajrayana teaches how to change negativity into compassion and wisdom.

CHRISTIAN MEDITATION

Christian meditation has its beginnings in Jesus. Scripture tells us he fasted and prayed in the desert for forty days and forty nights.

RELIGION & MODERN CULTURE

MORE KOANS

One monk said to the other, "The fish has flopped out of the net! How will it live?" The other said, "When you have gotten out of the net, I'll tell you."

A monk said to the master, "I have just entered this monastery. Please teach me." "Have you eaten your breakfast?" the master asked. "Yes, I have," replied the student. "Then you had better wash your bowl."

A monk asked the teacher, "Is there any great spiritual teaching that has not been preached to the people?" The teacher said, "There is." "What is the truth that has not been taught?" "Nothing," the teacher replied.

A young monk asked his teacher, "What is the true spiritual nature of life?" His teacher picked up a bowl of water and threw it in the student's face, saying, "Go wash out your mouth!"

If you meet a person on the path, do not greet him with either words or silence. How will you greet him?

A monk, taking a bamboo stick, said to the people, "If you call this a stick, you fall into the trap of words, but if you do not call it a stick, you contradict facts. So what do you call it?" At that time a monk in the assembly came forth. He snatched the stick, broke it in two, and threw the pieces across the room.

RELIGION & MODERN CULTURE

Following his example, in the third and fourth centuries, a group known as the Desert Fathers lived alone in Palestine and Egypt, spending much time in prayer as they learned to be aware of God's presence. They wanted to experience God directly. From these monks and hermits came a rich Christian tradition of *mysticism* and meditation. Today, the Christian form of meditation is also known as "contemplative prayer."

One form of prayer from the Christian contemplative tradition is called "The Jesus Prayer." The worshipper repeats (either aloud or silently), "Lord Jesus Christ, Son of the living God, have mercy on me, a sinner." As the phrase is repeated, it sinks deeper and deeper into the soul.

The contemplative Christian tradition continued for more than a thousand years. Later Christians famous for their meditative spirituality include Teresa of Avila, Julian of Norwich, and John of the Cross. Their mystical spirituality included visions and dreams. Although the church did not officially allow women to serve as priests, female mystics were highly respected, and they taught spiritual practices to both women and men.

Quakers continued the Christian tradition of meditation. They emphasized that Christ was an "inner light" that would guide those who listened in silence.

MUSLIM & JEWISH FORMS OF MEDITATION

Around 800 BCE, a movement called Sufi emerged within Islam, a word that comes from its disciples' practice of wearing wool (*suf* in Arabic). The earliest Sufis would spend almost all their waking hours in prayer. They also practiced asceticism, avoided comforts, and went without food or sleep for long periods of time. All Muslims believe mortals will see God after death, but Sufis do not wish to wait that long. Hence, the Sufi expression, "Die before you die," which means, "Experience God in this life." The classic Sufi form of meditation is called *zikr*, which involves a repeated phrase, usually one of God's names, combined with deliberate breathing exercises.

Kabbalah, Jewish mysticism, became well known in the Middle Ages, though it may have existed earlier. This spiritual tradition grew out of the Jewish love for the Hebrew scriptures. Practitioners believe hidden meanings can be found in the letters that form the words of the Torah (Jewish scripture). By meditating on these, Kabbalah teaches one can encounter God directly. Recently, the pop singer Madonna has become a follower of Kabbalah, and Jewish mysticism is experiencing a new wave of interest in the United States.

MEDITATION GOES MAINSTREAM

For a long time, Eastern forms of spirituality were unknown in the West. In the 1800s, however, famous American writers Ralph Waldo Emerson and Henry David Thoreau translated Hindu and Buddhist texts, and in 1893, two Buddhist masters came to the World Congress of Religions in Chicago, Illinois. A Jewish businessperson, Charles T. Strauss, became the first citizen of the United States to adopt Buddhism in America.

In the 1950s and early 1960s, famous American writers Alan Ginsberg and Jack Kerouac became familiar with Buddhist writings. They helped Eastern spirituality gain acceptance among the "Beat" crowd, who were the forerunners of the hippies. With the 1960s, great numbers of young people began to seek spiritual experiences in ways that were nontraditional from a *Western* perspective. Along with experimenting with drugs, TM became popular. Participants in the civil rights movement who followed Dr. Martin Luther King Jr. realized that

"*Our life is shaped by our mind; we become what we think. Suffering follows an evil thought as the wheel of the cart follows the oxen that draw it.*"

—*saying of the Buddha, from the* Dhammapada

WISDOM FROM THE DESERT FATHERS

A brother who was insulted by another brother came to Abba Sisoes and said to him: "I was hurt by my brother, and I want to avenge myself." The old man tried to console him and said: "Don't do that, my child. Leave vengeance to God." But he said: "I will not quit until I avenge myself." Then the old man said: "Let us pray, brother," and standing up, he said: "O God, we no longer need you to take care of us since we now avenge ourselves." Hearing these words, the brother fell at the feet of the old man and said: "I am not going to fight with my brother any more. Forgive me, Abba."

—from *Desert Wisdom*, by Henri J. M. Nouwen

spiritual practices could give them the strength to struggle for justice in a nonviolent way. At the same time, Catholic monk Thomas Merton brought renewed interest in contemplation into Christian circles. His friendship with Thich Nhat Hanh helped begin a dialogue between Christian and Buddhist spiritual practitioners. It took several decades, but the spiritual openness of the 1960s grew into the varied American spiritual landscape of today.

Chapter 3

MEDITATION TODAY

Sean Toomey has begun to notice some changes in his life. He has a greater sense of well-being and an improved self-image, and he relates better to family members and coworkers. The benefit he most enjoys is a deeper awareness of the presence of God. Meanwhile, Stephen Pierce says he now experiences a tremendous flow of creative energy. Olive Vayghan suffers less from headaches, and she is more relaxed. Clare Dooley has more energy and better health.

What do these people have in common? They all practice TM.

According to Dr. Dean Ornish, president and director of the Preventive Medicine Research Institute, "meditation is power." He believes that whatever a person does, meditation can help them do it better.

For thousands of years people have practiced meditation. Many major religions speak of its importance. Nonetheless, it was not popular in the Western world until a well-known band brought it from the East. The Beatles traveled to India to become students of the Maharishi Mahesh Yogi. They learned the practice of TM and brought it to the West. Since then, TM has become widely popular.

MEDITATION & THE MIND

Meditation is a form of concentration. It is the practice of focusing the mind and paying attention. The purposes of meditation are to quiet the brain, open the heart, and connect with a higher source. In his book *Love & Survival*, Dean Ornish tells of the benefits he believes meditation brings:

> First, a person gains more power when they can focus their awareness. When a person focuses their mind, they concentrate better. When they concentrate better, they perform better. Whatever a person does, they will do it more effectively when they meditate. Second, meditation can magnify the five senses. When a person concentrates on something, it is more enjoyable. Anything enjoyable—music, art, or food—can be enhanced by meditation. Third, a person can experience more peace, joy and a sense of well being. Meditation helps quiet the mind. Fourth, a person may feel a connection with creation. They may be more open to a spiritual experience.

Recent research has shown that meditation can have dramatic effects on the body. Studies have demonstrated that meditating for even a short time increases alpha waves (relaxed brain waves) and decreases anxiety

GLOSSARY

analytical: The act of separating things into their individual elements in order to study them.

linear: Develop sequentially from the obvious without using in-depth understanding.

and depression. Researchers at Harvard Medical School found that meditation activates the part of the brain that controls the autonomic nervous system, which includes the digestive system and blood pressure. Stress can cause damage such as digestive problems, heart disease, and infertility. Meditation helps calm these systems.

Meditation comes in many forms. All of them involve focusing the mind to quiet it. In many forms of meditation, the goal is to stop the thoughts. Teachers of meditation believe that when a person stops his thoughts, he can open up to another world of experiences and perceptions.

CONCENTRATIVE MEDITATIONS

In the 1960s, TM centers began showing up in every major city. Since then, hundreds of studies have proven its physical and emotional

> *"Hurry is not of the Devil; it is the Devil."*
> —*Psychiatrist C. G. Jung*

benefits. It is simple to do, and most people find it immediately gratifying. The TM method involves repeating a Sanskrit word as a special mantra. TM instructors believe they must choose the mantra for a student, but studies done by Herbert Benson, a research doctor at Harvard, have shown that it does not really matter what word is used. These studies found that any pleasant sound repeated in the way TM teachers instruct will create a very deep relaxation response. Usually a mantra consists of one, two, or three syllables. Some common mantras are "Allah," "Jehovah," "Rama," and "ohmmm."

A person wanting to meditate in the TM method should find a quiet place, sit with her back straight, eyes closed, and take a couple of slow, deep breaths. She will begin to recite the mantra to herself, repeating the word at a comfortable pace. After twenty minutes (or whatever time she has set), she will stop, and open her eyes. The exercise is finished. Maharishi Mahesh Yogi suggests that a person meditate for twenty minutes in the morning and another twenty minutes in the evening.

Another common form of meditation is one using the breath. Meditators in the Buddhist tradition sometimes clasp their hands on their stomachs and silently mark the rising and falling of their stomachs in relation to their breathing. Being aware of your breath coming and leaving your nostrils helps you to be mindful. Stephan Bodian, former editor in chief of *Yoga Journal*, writes, "Mindful awareness of what you are doing and experiencing can confer tremendous benefits," including greater focus, an experience of effortlessness, reduced stress, increased enjoyment of the fullness of life, deeper connections with loved ones and friends, and openness to the spiritual dimensions of life.

RELIGION & MODERN CULTURE

"Transcendental Meditation opens the awareness to the infinite reservoir of energy, creativity and intelligence that lies deep within everyone."
—*Maharishi Mahesh Yogi*

VISUALIZATION MEDITATION

Visualization is a form of meditation in which one uses an internal image to help open the heart and quiet the mind. Jonathan Robinson, author of *The Complete Idiot's Guide to Awakening Your Spirituality*, recommends a simple visualization exercise he calls the Pure Love Meditation.

First, get comfortable with peaceful music playing in the background. Take a deep breath, holding it and then exhaling with a slow, long sighing sound, and repeat three or four times. Focus on a person or animal for whom you feel love and affection. Picture him in your mind and imagine him giving you a loving look. As you breathe slowly, fill your heart with loving thoughts of him. When the music ends keep feeling the glow in your heart. Doing this in silence is acceptable also—whichever makes a person feel more peaceful. A shorter version of this exercise is to take a deep breath, think of a person you love, and release your breath slowly. The Institute of Heart Math has done studies showing that focusing on feelings of love and appreciation for even a minute can reduce stress hormones for several hours.

Sharon Salzberg, an American Buddhist teacher, tells in her book *Lovingkindness* of the time she spent at a retreat in which she did nothing else except extend loving kindness to herself for seven days, from morning to night. She found the experience very boring and felt that her time was wasted until an event happened the day she was leaving. She dropped a glass jar, which shattered all over the floor. Instead of being mad at herself, as she would have been normally, her response was, "You're really a klutz, but I love you." Something good did come from her meditating.

The forgiveness exercise found in *Meditation for Dummies* by Stephan Bodian helps dissolve resentment, guilt, and hurt, and helps open people's hearts to themselves and others. Begin by sitting in a chair in a relaxed state with your eyes closed. Remember words, actions, and thoughts for which you have never been able to forgive yourself or someone else. Allow yourself to feel the pain you or someone else caused you. Talk to yourself—forgiving yourself or the other person with words such as "For all of the mistakes you've made and the suffering you've caused—I forgive you. I know you have learned from this and its time to move on. May you be happy and peaceful. I accept you back into my heart." If it is another person you need to forgive, use appropriate words for her. Maybe someone else needs to forgive you; imagine asking for his forgiveness. If you have closed your heart to someone, feel the layers of resentment and pain that have built up; say words of forgiveness to them, feel your heart opening up to them again. End by breathing deeply and resting your attention in your heart. Then go about your day.

"All of the masters of meditation strive to awaken us to the unexplored inner regions that are just as real as the physical world we know so well. They tell us of exciting possibilities for new life and freedom. They call us to the adventure, to be pioneers in this frontier of the Spirit."

—*Richard J. Foster, author*

Many exercises use visualization—images inside one's mind—to bring peace through meditation. Studies have shown that forgiving oneself or others helps a person emotionally, spiritually, and physically.

CONTEMPLATIVE MEDITATION

Another form of meditation is contemplative meditation, or contemplative prayer. In his book, *Celebration of Discipline: The Path to Spiritual Growth,* Richard Foster says: "Meditation has always stood as a classical and central part of Christian devotion." There are very few contemporary Christian teachers on the subject; most of the serious writings on contemplative meditation are centuries old. According to Christian belief, the practice dates back to the life of Jesus.

Foster believes that Christian meditation is different from Eastern meditation in the sense that it is not just an attempt to empty the mind, but an attempt to empty it so that it can be filled with God. He also feels that, "meditation is the one thing that can sufficiently redirect our lives so that we can deal with human life successfully." Meditating on nature is one way of getting closer to God. Foster suggests choosing

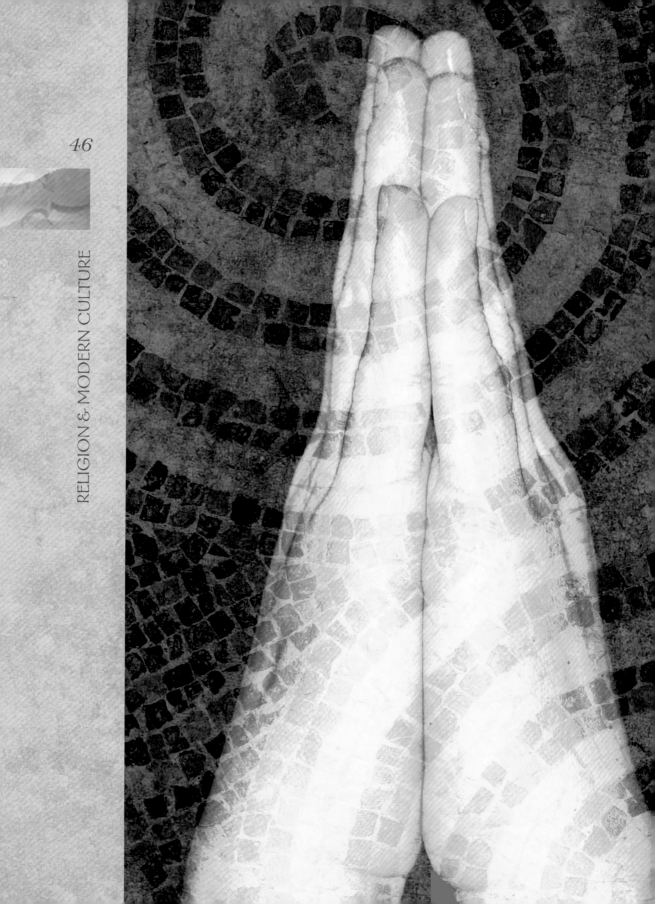

> *"Every morning, when we wake up, we have twenty-four brand-new hours to live. What a precious gift! We have the capacity to live in a way that these twenty-four hours will bring peace, joy, and happiness to ourselves and others."*
>
> —*Thich Nat Hanh, Vietnamese Buddhist monk*

something in creation—a tree, bird, cloud, or plant. Each day ponder it carefully and prayerfully so that God can show himself through his creation. The old mystics called this form of contemplation "discovery of God in His creatures."

Another form of contemplation described in Foster's book is meditation on scripture. He writes that all the masters considered meditation on scripture "as the normal foundation for the interior life." He suggests taking a single event in scripture, like the resurrection, or a parable, a few verses, or even just a word, and allowing it to take root in you. Involve all your senses: hear the sea, feel the sun on your back, experience the hunger in your stomach, taste the salt in the air. Foster says one should enter the story as an active participant, remembering that since Jesus lives in the Eternal Now and is not bound by time, one can actually meet the living Christ in her meditation. One Christian theologian recommended living with your scripture passage during the day and even taking a whole week to meditate on a single part of scripture.

Yet another method of contemplative meditation is to think about the answers to a certain question. This can bring about a deeper level of awareness and a positive feeling. Jonathan Robinson has found over the years that three questions in particular are effective in bringing awareness to a situation or helping to change a person's feelings: What do I need to do or know to experience more peace now? What could I be thankful for? Who loves me and whom do I love?

ADVICE FROM A FAMOUS BUDDHIST

Thich Nhat Hanh is a Vietnamese Buddhist monk who teaches mindfulness and social responsibility. He created and headed the Buddhist peace delegation to the Paris peace talks during the Vietnam War, and he worked so unceasingly for peace in his country that Martin Luther King Jr. nominated him for a Nobel Peace Prize. Thich Nhat Hanh suggests saying the following verse silently to enhance mindfulness and to turn conscious breathing into a chance to relax and take pleasure from life:

Breathing in, I calm my body.

Breathing out, I smile.

Dwelling in the present moment, (breathe in)

I know this is a wonderful moment. (breathe out)

Begin by taking a slow, deep breath. Ask yourself the question several times. If you are feeling stressed about something, ask yourself, "What should I do to feel more peaceful now?" You may receive the thought to let go of the tension in your body. You will then focus on how tense your body feels, and because you are aware of it, you can consciously begin to let go of it. You should begin to feel more peaceful.

"Every breath we take, every step we make, can be filled with peace, joy, and serenity. We need only to be awake, alive in the present moment."

—*Thich Nat Hanh, Vietnamese Buddhist monk*

When a person contemplates the other two questions, he can help himself feel more gratitude and love. When he asks himself, "What could I feel thankful for?" he can focus on many things: health, food, friends, and family. When he focuses on how fortunate he is, he will feel more thankfulness, gratitude, and peace. When asking the question, "Who loves me and whom do I love?" the person can remember an experience of being in love. Thinking about this will give him a feeling of love that will warm his heart and bring more peace.

In Zen Buddhism, koan meditation is a form of contemplative meditation. Since a koan has no clear answer, it stimulates thought. A Zen teacher will give a student a question the student cannot solve by rational, **linear**, or **analytical** thinking. Some answers come from intuition—from deep in the subconscious. They come from looking inward. The student will meditate on the koan, and when he has an answer, he will hurry to the teacher and give the answer. Usually it is wrong at first, so he will go back and meditate on it more. Suddenly, at some point, the answer will come to the student. It will seem very simple and clear and sometimes funny—how could he have overlooked this answer? He will go to the teacher and tell him the answer. The teacher may smile and acknowledge his success, and then give him another question or koan.

The most famous Zen koan is, "What is the sound of one hand clapping?" Perhaps by using your mind to concentrate, visualize, or contemplate, you will come up with the answer. However, you might need to skip rational thinking and just use your intuition. Deep in your subconscious, you probably already know the answer; most certainly, it involves peace, joy, and happiness.

CONNECTIONS BETWEEN MIND, BODY, & SPIRIT

The subject of an experiment was so allergic to the oil of the Japanese lacquer tree that if one of its leaves simply brushed against his arm, a rash would develop. A scientist rubbed one arm of the blindfolded subject with the lacquer tree leaf and the other arm with the harmless leaf of a chestnut tree. The subject knew he was being rubbed by both leaves, but he did not know which was which. Before long, the subject's right arm turned red and developed itchy welts while the left arm remained unaffected. Imagine the surprise of the subject when he found out that his left arm was the one that had been rubbed with the Japanese lacquer tree leaf.

"The man who opts for revenge should dig two graves."
—*Chinese Proverb*

Imagine you have Parkinson's disease, and your condition has deteriorated so that your walk is only a shuffle and your hands shake so much that you cannot grasp a pencil. You are given an experimental surgery. Your walk greatly improves, and your grip returns. Most of us would declare it a near miracle—until we found that the operation was a fraud: the surgeon had only drilled a small hole in your skull and then closed it.

These two examples of the power of the mind over the body are at the start of a *Newsweek* article by Herbert Benson, Julie Corliss, and Geoffrey Cowley. The article suggests that the power of our thoughts is immense.

The idea that thoughts and feelings affect our bodies is not new. Lately, however, scientists have had a heightened interest in studying the effects of mental states on our bodies. They are seeing that anxiety and depression, or love and tranquility, are not merely feelings but are psychological states that influence our bodily health as surely as obesity or physical fitness does. According to *Newsweek*'s September 27, 2004, issue, the federal government's Integrated Immune Neural Program wil spend $16 million on mind–body research in the year 2005; private companies will spend millions more.

At the same time, the medical world is also exploring the influence of spirituality on the physical body. More than half the medical schools in the United States have courses on spirituality and medicine. *Newsweek* magazine took a poll and found that 72 percent of Americans would welcome a conversation with their doctor about faith. Many believe that prayers for a physical cure can be effective even when science says a cure is impossible. There is also a growing belief in the medical community that what happens in a person's mind and perhaps soul can be as important to the health as what happens on the physical, cellular level.

STUDY ON TWINS & SPIRITUALITY

A famous twins study at the University of Minnesota beginning in 1979 had some interesting results. Fifty-three pairs of identical twins and thirty-one pairs of fraternal twins separated at birth were the subjects. The identical twins were found to be twice as likely as fraternal twins to believe similarly about spiritual matters. How often the twins attended church seemed to be taught by their environments—but whether or not the twins chose to believe in God in the first place seemed hardwired into their genes. Twin studies done later in Virginia and Australia found similar results.

PATHWAYS THAT LINK EMOTIONS TO HEALTH

Ninety years ago, Harvard psychologist Walter Cannon recognized that when faced with danger—real or imagined, physical or emotional—our bodies react with increased heart rate, blood pressure, breathing rate, and muscle tension. Studies have shown that these stress responses involve inflammatory chemicals and hormones that are fine in small doses. When we experience them often, however, they can cause many

ailments—from headaches to heart attacks. Studies have shown that 60 to 90 percent of visits to the doctor are stress related. Therefore, reducing stress is a foremost priority in maintaining health.

According to a new government study, almost half of all Americans used some type of mind–body intervention during 2002. The practices ranged from deep breathing to hypnosis, guided imagery, muscle relaxation, and meditation. Almost half of the people studied used the oldest and most basic mind–body practice—prayer.

Experts are beginning to see the effects of a number of soothing emotional experiences on physical healing. Researchers at UCLA have found that optimism in men with HIV is connected to a stronger immune cell function. A Duke University study has shown that religious people have a lower incidence of illness and hospitalization. Studies at Harvard have demonstrated the beneficial effects of deep relaxation.

The body produces nitric oxides when it is deeply relaxed. These chemicals help to overcome cortisol and other hormones produced when we feel stress. The calming effects of prayer, deep-breathing exercises, and meditation can go a long way to help reduce the effects of daily stress. Meditation may not be able to cure cancer, but it can help the cancer patient feel less fear, and that in itself may help the healing process. Prayer is not a substitute for a healthy diet and prescribed medication, but it can increase a person's quality of life.

THE BENEFITS OF FORGIVENESS

"The most selfish thing you can do for yourself is to forgive someone," says Dr. Dean Ornish who, according to *Newsweek*, is "America's all-purpose lifestyle guru." This is not an easy thing for many of us to do. Maybe you remember an unfaithful boyfriend or girlfriend, a friend who betrayed you, or a parent who messed up your life. You wonder how you could ever forgive them.

"With all your science, can you tell me how it is that light comes into the soul?

—*Henry David Thoreau*

Here is one person's story of forgiveness from A Campaign for Forgiveness Research Web site: In the summer of 1976, while Marietta and Bill Jaeger were camping with their five children in the Badlands National Forest, their seven-year-old daughter, Susie, was kidnapped. For a full year, the police worked on the case. The family was grief-stricken. People surrounding the case spoke in vicious terms about the abductor, calling him inhuman. According to the Web site, "something within Marietta began to shift as the days of waiting turned into weeks. . . . Marietta heard a voice." She believed she heard God telling her not to feel this way about the kidnapper. Thinking about this message, the weight on her chest began to disappear, and the tension in her stomach lessened. This was the beginning of her commitment to release her anger and to find forgiveness for the abductor. A year after the crime, the kidnapper called the Jaegers' home. Marietta had spent months praying for the ability to forgive, and so she was able to communicate genuine compassion for the man as she spoke with him. She kept him on the line for an hour. Because of this, the police were able to track the man and catch him. His name was David Meirhoffer, and he confessed to killing Susie Jaeger a week after kidnapping her. He also confessed to kidnapping and killing other children. A short time later, he committed suicide. It would be understandable if Marietta changed her decision to forgive this criminal after she learned of her daughter's death—but she did not. Her husband, however, was never able to let go of his anger. He suffered for years with bleeding ulcers and died of a heart attack at age fifty-six. Meanwhile, Marietta began a speaking campaign around the country telling of her experience of learning to forgive. She befriended the mother of David Meirhoffer. Together they visited the graves of their children.

According to *Newsweek* magazine, September 27, 2004, the subject of forgiveness is one of the hottest topics of research today, with more than 1,200 published studies. Research shows that the state of unforgiveness includes emotions such as anger, hostility, resentment, and fear. These feelings cause the body to respond with increased blood pressure and a change in hormones. These physical responses are linked to cardiovascular disease, lower immunity to disease, and impaired neurological function and memory. When a person forgives, these stressors are relieved. Everett Worthington, executive director of A Campaign for Forgiveness, says that every time a person fails to forgive, they are more likely to develop some kind of health problem.

The author of *Dare to Forgive*, Dr. Edward M. Hallowell, tells us that forgiveness is a complex process that has to be cultivated. He recommends getting help through friends, a therapist, or prayer. Contrary to some thinking, forgiveness is not excusing or condoning what the other person has done. Instead, it is letting go of your own suffering, says Dr. Ornish. In the words of Marietta Jaeger, "If you remain vindictive, you give the criminal another victim . . . anger, hatred and resentment would have taken my life as surely as Susie's life was taken."

THE RELAXATION RESPONSE

Over the last thirty years, many studies have proved the benefits of the relaxation response. This is a state in which a person's heart and breathing rate slow down, her muscles become less tense, and her blood pressure drops. Studies have documented that when middle school students learned the relaxation response, their work habits, grades, and cooperation with others improved. When a person has become comfortable with the technique, it can be a helpful tool in overcoming everyday stresses.

Dr. Herbert Benson, president of the Mind Body Medical Institute in Boston and Associate Professor of Medicine at Harvard, and Julie

Corliss, a medical writer at Harvard Medical School, wrote an article in the September 27, 2004, *Newsweek* outlining three simple techniques for starting the relaxation response:

• *Meditation*: Pick a prayer or short phrase from your belief system such as "The Lord is my Shepherd" or "Peace." From your feet to your head relax your muscles. Inhale slowly, and as you exhale, say your word or phrase silently to yourself. Do this exercise for ten to twenty minutes. When finished, sit quietly for a minute. Just five minutes of deep relaxation can help calm and refresh a person.

• *Paced respiration*: Inhale slowly, causing your stomach to extend. As you exhale, silently say the number five to yourself. Pause briefly and take another slow breath. As you exhale, think the number four. Count down at your own pace to one. Do this for ten to fifteen minutes in the morning and evening.

• *Repetitive activities*: A person does not have to be sitting silently to start the relaxation response. It can be done while walking, running, playing a musical instrument, or doing simple repetitive tasks such as crocheting or knitting.

THE GOD GENE

Scientists have wondered if spirituality might come from our DNA. Does nature or nurture make some people more spiritual than others? Molecular biologist Dean Hamer, chief of gene structure at the National Cancer Institute, recently published a book, *The God Gene: How Faith Is Hardwired into Our Genes*. According to *Time* magazine, October 25, 2004, Hamer says, "I'm a believer that every thought we think and every feeling we feel is the result of activity in the brain. I think we follow the

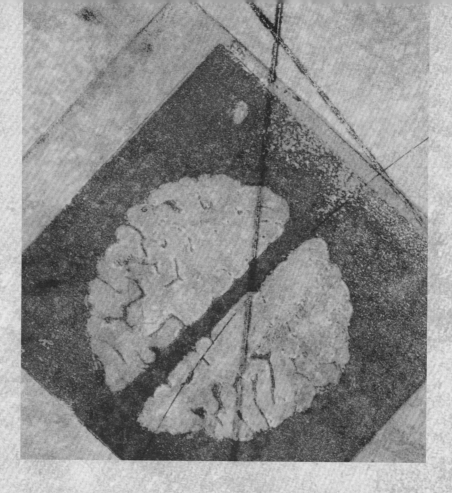

basic laws of nature, which is that we're a bunch of chemical reactions running around in a bag."

What started as a survey on smoking and addiction grew into a spirituality study. Among the traits his smoking survey measured was one known as self-transcendence. This consists of three traits: the ability to get lost in an experience, openness to things not literally provable, and a feeling of connectedness to a larger universe. These traits come close to measuring what it feels like to be spiritual. Hamer ranked his participants from least to most spiritually interested. He then tried to find the DNA responsible for the differences in spirituality.

He found that those with the nucleic acid cytosine in a particular spot on the gene known as VMAT2 were more spiritually inclined than the others were. *Time* quotes Hamer, "A single change in a single base in the middle of the gene seemed directly related to the ability to feel self-transcendence." Hamer points out that the gene he found is not the only one to influence spirituality. Hundreds of genes could effect belief in God. He also stresses that the gene he identified relates to spirituality, not how a person chooses a religion.

God is a concept that appears in cultures all over the globe, even in remote cultures. To some, this is a strong indication that the knowledge of God might be preloaded into our brains. If God made human beings, why wouldn't he have included, as *Time* magazine put it, "a genetic chip" that would make us able to think about him?

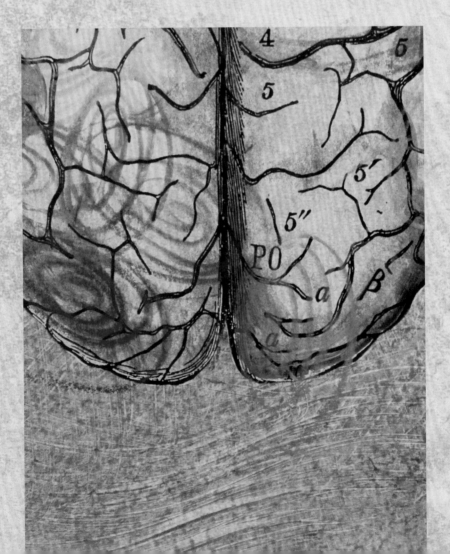

Chapter 5

BODY-CENTERED SPIRITUAL PRACTICES

A college girl's anxiety attacks began to occur randomly in her junior year. They felt like a 500-pound weight on her chest making it almost impossible to breathe, and she never knew when to expect them. Her doctor suggested a medication to help with the panic attacks, but the young woman did not want to go that route. She began to live in constant fear, afraid to sleep at night for fear her breathing would become short or her heart would begin to flutter.

She hoped the attacks would go away but they didn't—not until she began practicing Bikram yoga at least four times a week. (Bikram is the founder of a worldwide yoga college in India.) Her attacks became less frequent and less intense. Weeks passed without an attack. When they came, she learned how to breathe through them without feeling like her body was out of control. Yoga gave her a new lease on life.

Spiritual practices have three basic pathways: the emotions, the mind, and the body. Experts say people need to develop all three areas in order to be holistically healthy. Many eat unhealthily, exercise little, and stress too much. One-third of the U.S. population is obese; in Canada, 10 to 25 percent of teens and 20 to 50 percent of adults have weight problems. People who care for *all* aspects of their health experience more of a general sense of peace, and feel better emotionally and spiritually.

For thousands of years various spiritual traditions have used the body to make people more mentally and spiritually aware. During the last forty years, these methods have become better known in the United States and Canada.

THE ANCIENT ART OF YOGA

Some claim yoga is the oldest science of life. People may have practiced yoga as far back as five to eight thousand years ago in India. Although yoga can be traced back to the Rig-Veda, the oldest Hindu scriptures (2000–1500 BCE), the *Bhagavad Gita* (800–1000 BCE) is considered to be the principal yoga text. Scholars believe Pantanjali, an Indian sage, wrote the Yoga Sutra somewhere between the second and third centuries BCE. The Yoga Sutra contains 195 statements still used as a philosophical guidebook for yoga practices.

Yoga means union. The purpose of yoga is to join with the God energy inside of us. Eastern philosophers believe that in uniting with this energy, practitioners can step off the cycle of death and rebirth. They believe that true freedom is leaving the temporary earthly life behind. If a person spends her life under the care of a yoga master, and devotes herself to yoga practices, she might reach this ultimate goal of union. Yoga is not a religion but a philosophy. It is not necessary to give up your own religious beliefs to practice yoga.

GLOSSARY

meridians: A group of invisible longitudinal lines or pathways on the body, along which acupuncture points are distributed.

The ancient art of yoga has become a modern popular practice in North America. A study in 2001 by the Sporting Goods Manufacturers Association showed that the number of people who practiced tai chi or yoga had grown to 9.2 million in the United States. One Canadian Web site, yogafinder.com, lists nearly two hundred towns and cities with a yoga center. The *Yoga Journal* released figures in 2003 from the Harris interactive poll that showed 15 million people in the United States practice yoga. However, according to sociologist Paul Ray, a board member of Gaiam, the largest wellness industry conglomerate, 28 million people in the United States practiced yoga in 2003. Although these figures differ, possibly due to the method in which the statistics were gathered, we can see that the number of yoga practitioners is rising in the West.

One of the most interesting yoga-type centers in Canada is in Vancouver, an International Laugh Club started by Dr. Madan Kataria. He started the clubs in India ten years ago, and they have spread to many countries since. Katarias's laughing exercises come from a yoga technique called Kaphalbhati. According to practitioners, a person who

laughs often cannot help but have a good attitude. Medical science has proven many physical and emotional benefits of laughter.

Many benefits are claimed for yoga. It brings relaxation: gentle yoga stretches, breathing, and meditation help release tension. It increases concentration: the practice of balancing postures helps increase the focus of attention. It tones the body: when yoga postures are held, it creates isometric exercise, which tones even the inside organs. It promotes healing: yoga exercises the glands, organs, and endocrine system and increases circulation to stimulate and heal the body. Many people have given testimonials about the benefits of yoga. From the healing of anxiety attacks to scoliosis, people have benefited from this practice for centuries.

QIGONG—A VITAL FORCE

Sit up in a relaxed posture, take a slow deep breath, and rest your mind for a minute. You are practicing *Qigong* (pronounced "chi gong"). On any given day in China, thousands of people can be seen in parks practicing Qigong. They may be doing individual exercises or be exercising in large groups. It is not unusual to see a person in hospital pajamas doing a slow intent walk—a Qigong cancer-recovery exercise.

Qigong means breath or energy—*Qi*—combined with practiced body motions and mental focus—*gong*. Qigong is a sequence of motions combined with breathing that gives practitioners a balance of mind and emotion. Qigong practitioners believe that with much practice they can soak up and channel the energy of the universe to keep healthy. Doing so, they can help others to heal and grow spiritually. There are some hospitals in China where only Qigong treatments are used.

On the Internet there are listings for ninety-five groups and institutes in the United States, Canada, and other parts of the world that practice Qigong. Alternative medical practices are growing in Western

" [Karate] strives neither for victory or defeat, but for the perfection of the character of its practitioners."

—*Gichin Funakoshi, father of modern-day karate*

countries. A report developed by the Institute for Alternative Futures shows that health-care professionals in the United States trained in Oriental medicine will swell to 24,000 in 2010. Qigong is one of these medicinal practices.

Qigong has been called the grandparent of acupuncture, which originated in China, around the third century BCE, when Buddhism came to China from India and its secrets were shared with Qigong practitioners. Qigong was first written about in the *I Ching* in the twelfth century. It shares the view with acupuncture that the body has twelve **meridians** and eight vessels that flow like rivers of energy. These vessels keep the organs, tissues, and muscles healthy by feeding them energy. When one of them is blocked or does not have much energy, disease occurs. The meditations, movements, and visualizations of Qigong keep the flow of energy and oxygen at healthy levels. If a certain part of the body has become unhealthy, the movements can direct the flow of energy to that area. Buddhists believe the body can heal itself when it has a balanced flow of energy.

MARTIAL ARTS

Many movie fans are familiar with Bruce Lee, Chuck Norris, Steven Seagal, and David Carradine. These famous martial arts heroes are lethal yet cool, calm, and collected. The martial arts, however, are more related to the character of the Karate Kid, whose teacher demanded respect, patience, and discipline as he wiped the master's car over and over.

HOW TO DO THE POWER BREATH

Sit in a chair with your spine straight. Place the back of your hands near your shoulders, making a soft fist out of each hand. Inhale strongly through your nose and lift your arms straight over your shoulders. Exhale, bringing your hands next to your shoulders while powerfully letting out air through your nose. Repeat this form of breathing as strongly and as quickly as you can for a minute. Slow down or stop if you feel light-headed. Take a deep breath and then keep going at a comfortable pace. Once you have done this exercise for a full minute, take a last deep breath and hold it for twenty seconds or longer. Exhale making a slow, long, sighing sound. You should feel energy throughout your body.

Martial arts masters believe their disciplines began with an Indian Buddhist monk named Bodidharma who traveled from India to China in the year 526 CE. He found that the monks at the Shaolin Temple in Central China were physically very weak. They had spent much time meditating and not much time in physical movement, so he used his knowledge of Kataripayit, an ancient Indian fighting technique, mixed with religious practice to strengthen the monks. Traditionally, this was the beginning of martial arts.

During the period of history after Bodidharma, when weapons were outlawed, martial arts flourished. The Japanese word *karate* means "empty hands" or "to defend without weapons." For centuries, warrior classes were trained in the martial arts to defend others. In the mid-nineteenth century, these warrior classes were no longer needed, so the purpose of martial-arts training became self-development and spiritual growth.

Martial arts came to the United States after World War II. Soldiers in Okinawa learned the art and brought it home with them. A former sailor started the first martial arts school, called a *dojo*, in Phoenix, Arizona, in 1946. In the 1960s, judo gained popularity when it became an official sport in the 1964 Olympics. Chuck Norris became a title winner and a prominent figure in the martial arts world. Bruce Lee and Jackie Chan movies became huge successes and encouraged the popularity of martial arts even further.

Millions of North Americans practice the martial arts. In Canada, the Web site martialarts.ca lists 2,200 martial arts organizations throughout the country; martialarts.com lists over 15,000 schools in Canada and the United States. Martial arts aren't for everyone, though; some North Americans have turned to a slower form of physical discipline.

TAI CHI

Tai chi is a slow-motion exercise that large groups of people practice in hundreds of parks across China and more recently in many other parts of the world. Practitioners appear as though they are doing a dance in slow motion. It is a moving form of yoga and meditation. The Chinese believe the precise, slow, body movements harmonize the energy of the body with the energy of the universe. When focusing on each movement, the practitioner is supposed to become more relaxed, balanced, and connected to the energy of the cosmos.

Tai chi began as a martial art first taught by a teacher named Chang San-feng. However, further back in history the movements may have originated from a physician, Huantu'o, who taught his patients the movements of five creatures—the bear, tiger, deer, ape, and bird. He believed the body needed regular exercise to have a long and healthy life.

BREATHE, BREATHE, & BREATHE

Pranayama is one of the eight forms of yoga found in the ancient text of Patanjali's Yoga Sutras. It is the stretching, controlling, and restraint of breath. Prana means breath and is seen as not only what we breathe, but also as the energy filling the entire universe. There are many breathing exercises in Pranayama. One of them is the power breath. It has an energizing effect that can last for an hour.

Practicing mind/body movements has helped countless people enhance their physical, mental, and spiritual health for centuries. Dr. Norman Anderson, former director of the Office of Behavioral and Social Sciences Research at the National Institutes of Health, believes that our spiritual, mental, and physical selves are "inextricably linked." He says:

> Our beliefs, our emotions, our behavior, our thoughts, our family and cultural systems, as well as the environmental context in which we live, all are as relevant to our health as our genetic inheritance and our physiology.

Chapter 6

RELIGION & MODERN CULTURE

PRAYER

In the middle of the night, a young woman sits in a car with a friend, sobbing. She had an argument with her husband; he yelled that he was getting a divorce and threw her things out of the house. She ran out, fearing for her safety. Now, she can't stop crying, and her friend cannot find words to comfort her. Instead, the friend finds herself saying the words of the Lord's Prayer: "Our Father, which art in Heaven, hallowed be thy name." The distraught young woman joins her friend in mouthing the familiar words. Together, they pray the ancient words, over and over.

"God, grant me the serenity to accept the things I cannot change, courage to change the things I can and the wisdom to know the difference."

—*The Serenity Prayer (attributed to Reinhold Niebuhr)*

After a while, the young woman stops and looks at her friend. "Thanks," she says. "Those words really helped. I feel like I can make it now. I don't know what I'm going to do tomorrow, but I'm going to make it through this somehow." Like millions of others, she has found strength in prayer to help her through a crisis.

THE PREVALENCE OF PRAYER

More Americans pray than do yoga, or meditate, or go to church. Prayer is the most common form of spiritual practice. A survey by *U.S. News & World Report* in December 2004, found that 64 percent of Americans pray more than once a day. A Fox News survey taken almost the same time disclosed that less than one in ten Americans say they "never pray." Furthermore, a report conducted by cardiologists revealed that 97 percent of patients pray the night before undergoing heart surgery. Curiously, that is higher than the number of Americans who say they believe in God's existence. Apparently, when afraid, even atheists will take a chance on someone hearing their prayers.

A smaller—though still significant—percentage of Canadians practice daily prayer: a December 2004 *Toronto Sun* article stated that "An estimated 45% of Canadians pray every day." Curiously, that number is up 15 percent from a survey taken in 1992, in which only 30 percent of Canadians reported daily prayer. According to a 2002 study by Professor Reginald Bibby of the University of Lethbridge, 74 percent of Canadians say they pray at times.

MUSLIM PRAYER FOR PEACE

In the name of Allah, the beneficent, the merciful.

Praise be to the Lord of the Universe who has created us and made us

into tribes and nations

That we may know each other, not that we may despise each other.

If the enemy incline towards peace,

do thou also incline towards peace,

and trust God,

for the Lord is the one that heareth and knoweth all things.

And the servants of God,

Most gracious are those who walk on the Earth in humility,

and when we address them, we say "PEACE."

Prayer is essential to a wide variety of spiritual traditions. Christians recall Jesus's example of frequent prayer and the way he taught the Lord's Prayer to his disciples. The Hebrew scriptures record the prayers of King David, set to beautiful and timeless poetry in the Psalms.

If Christians and Jews have a long tradition of praying, what about Buddhists? According to the Buddha Dharma Education Society,

"Dear Jesus,
Help me to spread your fragrance everywhere I go.
Flood my soul with your spirit and life.
Penetrate and possess my whole being so utterly that my
life may only be a radiance of yours.
Shine through me and be so in me that every soul I come
in contact with may feel your Presence in my soul.
Let them look up and see no longer me but only Jesus.
Stay with me and then I shall begin to shine as You
shine, so to shine as you to be a light to others."

—*A prayer by Mother Teresa*

As Buddhism is a religion without a God, it might be asked who do Buddhists pray to? Or do they pray at all? The answer is that most Buddhists pray, but they are praying to the Buddha within themselves. They believe that the enlightened nature of the Buddha is their own real nature, which they have not yet been able to reach. So when they pray, it is to that deepest part of themselves.

Muslims follow five pillars of practice—actions that are essential to Muslim faith. The second pillar is prayer. Islam (which means obedience to Allah) requires the faithful to pray five times each day. In some large cities, including Washington and San Francisco, mosques announce times of prayer. Most Muslims in North America use their watches or other reminders to pray. In addition to formal prayer, Muslims talk informally with God, as do followers of most religions. An Islamic proverb says "to pray and to be Muslim are the same."

Prayer takes many forms. Some traditions emphasize memorized prayers, such as the Hail Mary or Our Father (the Lord's Prayer). Other traditions, such as Pentecostal Christianity, emphasize informal or "inspired" prayers.

Some religions, such as Islam and Hinduism, encourage praying prostrate (lying down) in humility before God. Other faiths, such as Judaism, pray while standing. Roman Catholic and Orthodox Christians sometimes pray kneeling in church. Some religions encourage believers to pray with head covered. Others teach it is more reverent to remove hats before prayer. Some people shout their prayers; a few pentecostal preachers literally scream their requests to God. Others utter their prayers silently.

THE PURPOSES OF PRAYER

PRAYERS OF PETITION

When in trouble, most people pray. As the expression goes, "There are no atheists in foxholes"—and there may not be any atheists taking end-of-year exams either! Prayers of petition—requests for some form of divine help—are very common. Sixty-five percent of people in the *U.S. News & World Report* survey said they pray for their health, most often regarding mental health or depression. Prayer services for healing are common in many churches. A 2004 survey by HC Research and the Jewish Theological Seminary of New York City found that 51 percent of medical doctors pray for their patients in groups, and 59 percent pray for their patients individually. Furthermore, 67 percent encourage their patients to pray.

A 2003 study conducted by Ipsos Reid, Canada's largest marketing survey company, determined that 75 percent of Canadians believe "God is an ever-present force in my life." A similar number, 73 percent, say that God is "there to be called upon in crisis."

Churches, synagogues, and mosques usually include prayer for national and international needs in their worship services. A survey taken in 2002 by the *Christian Science Monitor* asked, "To what extent do you

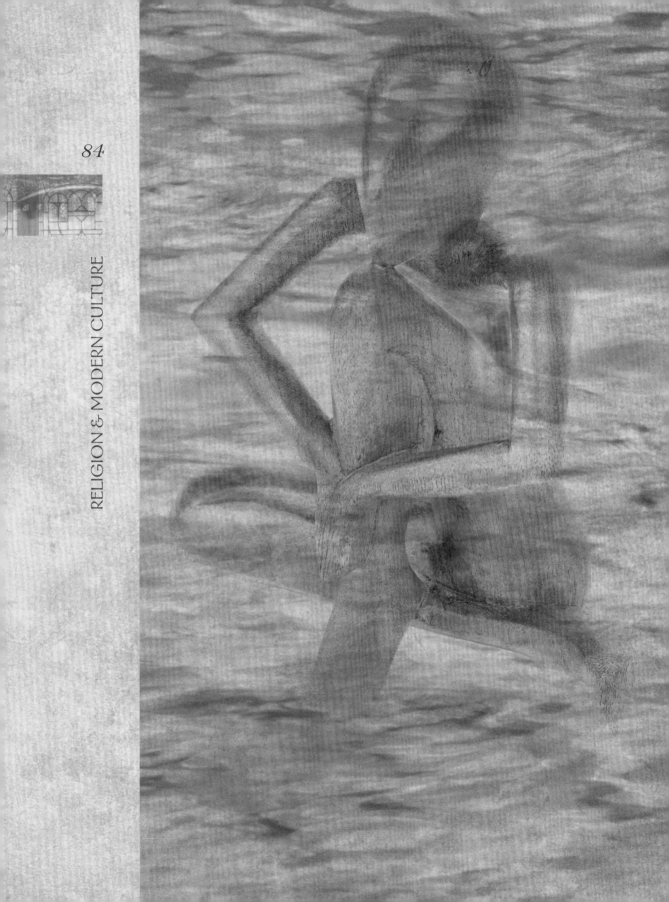

agree or disagree that prayer can have a positive impact on national or world events?" Eighty-eight percent of those responding said they agree or strongly agree. Seventy-one percent of those surveyed said they pray for "peace or an end to war."

PRAYERS OF THANKSGIVING

Many prayers—perhaps a majority—are for purposes other than requests. In the *U.S. News & World Report* survey, 67 percent of those who pray said, "In the past six months, their prayers have related to *giving thanks to God* all the time" (italics original). The New Testament verse that says "pray without ceasing" goes on to specify, "In everything give thanks" (1 Thessalonians 5:18).

The spiritual traditions of the Haudenosaunee (Iroquois) Native nations emphasize thanksgiving. Each morning, traditional Haudenosaunee people say a prayer called "the words that come before all other words." This prayer gives thanks to all elements of the universe and to their Creator. Beginning each day with a prayer of thanksgiving provides a positive perspective throughout the day for Native people who follow this path.

GUIDANCE FOR LIFE

A third aspect of prayer is guidance. Many believers would say prayer is a two-way conversation. God may not answer audibly, but they feel he directs their decisions by means of inward impressions or circumstances. In her book *The Joy of Listening to God*, Christian author Joyce Huggett writes: "When a person listens to God, God speaks, and when a man obeys, God works." Indeed, in the *Christian Science Monitor* survey, one of the most frequent reasons for prayer was to "seek guidance."

Some years ago, a *Guidepost* magazine article told how a boat captain felt "led" for reasons he could not understand to head his boat out into the open sea in a certain direction. As he did so, a small plane crashed

into the ocean, and the boat was able to rescue the plane's crew. If the captain had not responded to an inexplicable inner impulse, the crew would have perished. There are many similar reports of God communicating inwardly. People may attribute such reports to coincidence, psychic ability, or intuition. Many believers are convinced God guides them in such ways.

HOW DOES PRAYER WORK?

Prayer is like turning on the television set—one does not have to understand how it works in order to enjoy the experience. That is fortunate, because most people pray without thinking too deeply about it. Among those who do think about such things, there is disagreement as to what really happens in prayer.

The main question involves the type of prayer that makes petitions or requests. Most religious people believe strongly that "prayer changes things." Yet the question remains, how does that work? We might call the most common viewpoint "God sorts the requests." People who hold this perspective would say we mortals ask God for things, and God considers each request. Sometimes he says yes, sometimes he says no, and other times he says wait. According to this view, the "power" of prayer resides entirely with God.

Another perspective on prayer is summarized by Professor Walter Wink of Auburn Theological Seminary in New York City in his book *The Powers That Be*: "prayer changes what is possible to God." He believes God will not override human freedom; God must respect people's choices. However, when anyone prays, "A space opens in the praying person, permitting God to act without violating human freedom. The change in even one person thus changes what God can thereby do in the world."

Another view comes from Frank Laubach, a literacy teacher who taught thousands of people around the world how to read. He was also a devout Christian who taught and spoke frequently about prayer. Laubach believed prayer was a form of telepathy—a natural capability of the human mind to influence the physical world, not yet acknowledged by science. Prayer, in his view, was telepathy lined up with God's desires for the world. Laubach wrote:

> If people realize that telepathy is a fact though as yet not reduced to law—that ought to be the signal for a tremendous movement among Christian people to keep their thoughts right, to make them helpful every hour from morning to night. We may yet attempt to make the world over by the sheer force of good thoughts!

WHAT DOES PRAYER CHANGE?

Again, spiritual people of all faiths agree prayer changes things. Yet, there is disagreement regarding what things prayer changes. Religious scholars differ as to whether prayer changes God.

According to the classical Christian view, God is aware of the future as well as the past. Since God is "Alpha and Omega, beginning and end," some theologians believe that he exists outside of time. One writer compares God to a person reading a book. That book is the history of humanity. You and I are stuck on a certain page partway through the book; we cannot see the pages ahead of our time. God, however, can pick up and read the book at any point—including pages still "future" from our perspective.

This raises a question: if God has already written the future, what difference can prayer make? Gregory Boyd, professor of theology at Bethel College, is one of the foremost promoters of the "open view" of God. In Boyd's view, God knows everything that takes place in the world. However, God does not know exactly what will happen in the future, because the future does not yet exist. Thus, each prayer is actually "news" to God. Those who support the open view of God say that prayer is even more vital in their view than in the classical view. What will happen in the future depends in large part on whether or not people pray. In the open view, prayer changes God. Other theologians, however, believe that while God is outside time and thus "knows the future," he does not determine what will happen; human free will—and prayer—has real power to shape the course of events.

Religious thinkers agree on one thing—prayer changes the person praying. Famous Christian author C. S. Lewis writes, "I pray because I can't help myself. I pray because I'm helpless. I pray because the need flows out of me all the time, waking and sleeping. *It doesn't change God, it changes me*" (italics added). According to Judaism, Christianity, and Islam, the majority of problems in the world are the result of human evil. If prayer changes great numbers of people to do good, then prayer does indeed change the world.

CAN THE POWER OF PRAYER BE PROVEN?

A number of studies have attempted to prove the effectiveness of prayer. Researchers conducting a study at San Francisco General Hospital in 1988 reported that patients for whom others prayed needed only one-fifth as many antibiotics to recover from illness as did those who did not have anyone praying for them. Another study, done in 2001, claimed that women in South Korea receiving in vitro fertilization were twice as likely to succeed in having children if others prayed for them. In both of

RELIGION & MODERN CULTURE

these studies, subjects were unaware that people were praying for them. Both studies are controversial, as experts disagree whether researchers did these studies according to appropriate scientific standards.

At the same time, believers question whether prayer can be—or should be—proven. C. S. Lewis points out: "The thing we pray for may happen, but how can you ever know it was not going to happen anyway?" He goes on to assert, "Proof such as we have in the sciences can never be attained." At the same time, Lewis and others have no doubt God answers prayer. Prayer, after all, is something that comes straight from the heart, and the heart best knows its own realities.

PRAYER & PEACE

Prayer is not primarily about asking, nor is it about receiving things. Many people find that prayer gives them a deep sense of peace and confidence. Thomas Merton, a Catholic monk, and Richard Foster, a Protestant author, have both influenced Christians to appreciate contemplative prayer, which is similar to meditation. The focus is on experiencing God, rather than wrestling results from God. Contemplative prayer is silent, still, restful.

Sometimes, people who are in love with one another do not need to speak. Perhaps you have observed lovers at a table in a restaurant. They smile at one another, hold hands, make contact with their eyes. Romantic glances and tiny gestures can convey more passion than saying "I love you." In the same way, spiritual teachers have described contemplative prayer as silently enjoying the loving presence of God. Medieval mystic Saint Teresa of Avila described her prayer life as "an intimate friendship, a frequent conversation held alone with the Beloved." Perhaps that best describes the joy and satisfaction so many people experience in prayer.

LIVING PEACE

The late Viktor Frankl lived through hell on earth at the Auschwitz concentration camp. Frankl was one of the most famous psychotherapists of the twentieth century, and he helped countless people. More important, however, was his own experience of suffering during the Holocaust and the insights he gained from that experience. Gordon W. Allport describes Frankl's experience in the introduction to Frankl's book, *Man's Search for Meaning*.

As a long-time prisoner in bestial concentration camps he [Viktor Frankl] found himself stripped to naked existence. His father, mother, brother, and his wife died in camps or were sent to gas ovens, so that, excepting for his sister, his entire family perished in these camps. How could he—every possession lost, every value destroyed, suffering from hunger, cold and brutality, hourly expecting extermination—how could he find life worth preserving?

People in despair sometimes say, "No one else could understand the degree of my suffering, so no one can help me." Viktor Frankl is an important witness to people in such situations. At the beginning of *Man's Search for Meaning*, Frankl writes:

I had wanted simply to convey to the reader by way of concrete example that life holds a potential meaning under any conditions, even the most miserable ones. And I thought that if the point were demonstrated in a situation as extreme as that in a concentration camp, my book might gain a hearing. I therefore felt responsible for writing down what I had gone through, for I thought it might be helpful to people who are prone to despair.

According to Frankl, what is the secret to surviving through suffering? Frankl said, "There is nothing in the world, I venture to say, that would so effectively help one to survive even the worst conditions as the knowledge that *there is a meaning in one's life*" (italics added). He continues, "We may . . . find meaning in life even when confronted with a hopeless situation."

Many men and women have experienced inner peace, even in the midst of tragic or painful circumstances. The spiritual techniques described in this book—meditation, yoga, prayer—are all good.

GLOSSARY

paradoxical: Seemingly absurd or contradictory, but is or may be true.

However, many people find themselves in difficult circumstances when it is not possible to sit down in a lotus position for half an hour, or go through a stretching routine. There must be a way to experience peace even while busy at work or when caring for others. Inner peace must come from one's attitudes—from the ways one finds meaning in life. According to the great spiritual teachers of many religious traditions, it is possible to live at peace, even in times of crisis, poverty, or sickness.

LET GO OF ATTACHMENTS

Do you own your possessions—or do your possessions own you? According to great spiritual leaders, we experience peace when we let go of attachments.

The Buddha taught four Noble Truths. The first one says, "All life is suffering." The second Noble Truth says, "The cause of suffering is desire." Jack Maguire explains this concept in *Essential Buddhism*, "What causes us to suffer in an impermanent world is not the impermanence itself, but the desire burning within us to attach to things that are not lasting."

"Once we have the condition of peace and joy in us,
we can afford to be in any situation.
Even in the situation of hell,
We will be able to contribute our peace and serenity.
The most important thing is for each of us to have
some freedom in our heart,
some stability in our heart,
some peace in our heart.
Only then will we be able to relieve the suffering
around us."

—*Thich Nhat Hanh, Buddhist teacher*

In a similar vein, Jesus taught his followers, "The abundant life does not consist of material possessions." He pointed to humble natural objects—flowers and birds—as examples of the way God provides beauty and happiness on a daily basis. Jesus concludes, "So do not worry saying 'what shall we eat' or 'what shall we drink' or 'what shall we wear?' . . . your heavenly father knows that you need them [food, drink, and clothes]. But seek first his Kingdom and his righteousness, and all these things shall be yours as well."

Anthony De Mello was a Jesuit priest living in Calcutta. One day, he met a rickshaw driver named Rinesai. In his book *The Way to Love*, De Mello says that Rinesai, "although he was dying of a painful disease and was so poor that he had to sell his skeleton before he died, still was a man filled with faith and interior joy." De Mello concluded, "I was in the presence of a mystic who had rediscovered life. He was alive; I was dead." Inspired by this rickshaw driver, De Mello discovered principles that led to peace. He believed these principles were common to Christianity, Buddhism, and Hinduism. He wrote these concepts in *The Way to Love*.

De Mello begins by observing, "Take a look at the world and see the unhappiness around you and in you. Do you know what causes this unhappiness?" He suggests, "You have been programmed to be unhappy." He then makes a bold suggestion: "Almost every negative emotion you experience is the direct outcome of an attachment." According to De Mello, "An attachment isn't a fact. It is a belief, a fantasy in your head, acquired through programming." He explains:

> All you need to do is open your eyes and see that you do not really need the object of your attachment at all; that you were programmed, brainwashed into thinking that you could not be happy or you could not live without this particular person or thing.

Once a person has freed herself from attachments, she begins to enjoy people and things in a nondemanding, unselfish way. She appreciates people and things for their own sakes, not because of her needs. Thus, she experiences inner peace and happiness.

LIVE IN THE PRESENT

The book *Amazing Grace for Those Who Suffer* tells true stories of people who have lived through terrible events. For example, Janet Moylan lost her husband and ten-year-old daughter in a drowning accident. Mike and Kathie Clarey are parents whose eleven-year-old daughter was murdered. Carl Cleveland is a New Orleans lawyer who faced ten years in prison for false legal charges. All these people found hope and healing by relying on their faith.

"Life from the Center is a life of unhurried peace and power. It is simple. It is serene. It is amazing. It is triumphant. It is radiant. It takes no time, but it occupies all our time. And it makes our life programs new and overcoming. We need not get frantic. He is at the helm. And when our little day is done, we lie down quietly in peace, for all is well."

—*from* A Testament of Devotion

Many people believe they must remain unhappy because of some event in their past. They assume past events have power to keep them miserable. According to a number of spiritual guides, while past events—especially terrible events—do influence us, they do not have to enslave us. Spiritual teachers in a variety of traditions claim that people can experience inner peace by focusing on the present moment, rather than on the past or future. According to this view, a major cause of unhappiness comes from people mentally living in the past or the future, rather than in the now.

Similarly, some people think, "I will be happy in the future, once I have achieved such and such." This may take the form of longing for a partner: "I will become happy once I have a husband," or "I would be happy if I only had a girlfriend." It may involve dreams of success: "I would be happy if I had this job and made a certain amount of money." Likewise, "I'll be content once I own my own house or drive a really nice car."

Jesus taught his students: "Do not worry about tomorrow, for tomorrow will worry about itself. Each day has enough trouble of its own." Buddhism also emphasizes the importance of the present moment. In one Zen parable, a teacher asks, "What is the most important moment of your life?" The answer is, "This moment." The student cannot change his past, and the future does not exist. This moment is most important because it is the only moment the student can influence.

AT LEAST HELP SOMEONE ELSE

In the Jewish tradition, rabbis (teachers) communicate life-changing truths in story form. Jesus's parables are an example of rabbinic storytelling. The following story from Hassidic Judaism shows the importance of service in the spiritual life.

The Mitteler Rebbe was once in Homil visiting the well-known Chassid Reb Aizil of Homil on the intermediate days of Pesach (Passover). The Mitteler Rebbe's Hassidim in that town bemoaned to him that Reb Aizil was not befriending them and was only involved in his own life.

The Mitteler Rebbe asked him: "Why are you not reaching out to the youngsters in your community and teaching them Hassidus?" (Hassidic Jewish beliefs)

Reb Aizil responded: "If I don't have a quiet moment to work on myself, then how can I work with someone else?"

The Mitteler Rebbe replied: "Aizil, Aizil do as I do! When I see that I cannot have an effect on myself, should I then be a total waste? At least let me do a favor for someone else."

Faith as trust is trusting in the buoyancy of God. Faith is trusting in the sea of being in which we live and move and have our being.

—Marcus Borg

TRUST IN A GREATER POWER—& LIVE CONSTANTLY AWARE OF THE DIVINE PRESENCE

When they chose to depend on Divine power rather than on their own strength, countless men and women have discovered the power to free themselves of harmful habits, do things they did not believe they could do, and achieve inner peace.

More than 200,000 alcoholics have achieved freedom from addiction by following the famous Twelve Steps. The first step says, "We admitted we were powerless over alcohol—that our lives had become unmanageable." The second step goes on to say, "We came to believe that a power greater than ourselves could restore us to sanity."

Dependence on a greater power, rather than self-dependence, is what many religious people mean when they use the term "faith." In *The Heart of Christianity*, Professor of Religion Marcus Borg discusses various meanings of "faith." In a section describing "faith as trust," he writes:

> To help an adult class see this meaning of faith, my wife asked them, "How many of you have taught a small child to swim?" . . . all said their biggest challenge was getting the child to relax in the water. . . . Faith as trust is trusting in the buoyancy of God. Faith is trusting in the sea of being in which we live and move and have our being.

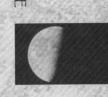

"I don't know what your destiny will be, but one thing I know: the only ones among you who will be really happy are those who will have sought and found how to serve."

—*Albert Schweitzer, medical missionary and humanitarian*

He concludes that "Growth in faith as trust casts out anxiety." Call it what you will—relying on a Higher Power, or faith—such an attitude can certainly make a difference.

A young man was struggling terribly with two kinds of cancer in his chest. Gasping for breath, in pain despite medication, he nonetheless tried to do the small things he enjoyed. He also made a serious effort to pray for other people. His mother was feeding him ice cream since he was too weak to feed himself. Attempting to inspire hope in her son, the mother said, "It's going to be all right."

The son replied, "Not *going to be* all right—it is all right." This young man had been through much surgery and suffering, but he had an unshakable trust in God. His faith enabled him to find pleasure in life, even on his most painful days.

A counselor is listening to a husband and wife in his office. They have come for help with their marriage. Despite the counselor's suggestions, words between the marital partners become harsher and louder. They accuse each other, yell at one another, and call each other nasty names. The counselor is saddened and frustrated; this is not going as he hoped. In the midst of this session, the counselor glances at a sign on his wall, "Bidden or not, God is present." The sign reminds him that the three of them are not alone. Mindful of the Divine presence, the counselor re-

A TIGER, TROUBLE, & PEACE

Another Buddhist story concerns a monk fleeing from a tiger. The ferocious beast chases him over the edge of a cliff. The monk grabs onto a small tree sticking out from the cliffside and holds on for life. Below him, is a long, deadly drop. In the story, the monk notices a strawberry growing on the branch. He takes and eats the strawberry, savoring its taste. Despite dangers above and below, he is now in a state of perfect peace. This story may seem extreme, but it illustrates an important spiritual concept. The monk chooses to focus on the present moment—rather than on the past or the future—and thus he achieves inner peace.

laxes. He prays a brief silent prayer, *Spirit of peace, help this unhappy couple.* As he does so, he notices the couple lowering their voices. They, too, sense a different atmosphere in the room.

In a variety of spiritual traditions, believers find they can maintain inner peace by "practicing the Divine presence." One cannot be constantly praying aloud, meditating, or practicing yoga. One can, however, maintain a constant sense of God's presence.

   In his book *A Testament of Devotion*, Quaker Thomas R. Kelly explains his own experience of the Divine presence. He writes, "There is a way of life so hid with Christ in God that in the midst of the day's busi-

ness one is inwardly lifting brief prayers, subdued whispers of adoration and of tender love to the Beyond that is within." He goes on to say, "One can live in a well-nigh continuous state of unworded prayer, directed toward God, directed toward people and enterprises we have on our heart."

HELPING OTHERS

Take a minute and ask yourself this question: Over the course of your life, when were the times you felt the most satisfied? It is likely that the times you recall feeling the greatest satisfaction were times when you were able to help another person. It is *paradoxical*, but almost all great spiritual traditions agree that people experience peace and happiness when they are helping other people. Ironically, if a person spent all her spare time seeking peace by meditation, yoga, or prayer, she might never find inner peace. True inner peace comes when one balances inward spiritual practices (like those described in this book) with serving others. Both Buddha and Jesus taught this principle.

A 1998 study of the effects of kindness to others found that self-esteem and sense of well-being increased by as much as 24 percent when people helped others. They did not have to make major lifestyle changes to make a difference; these people simply engaged in habitual acts of kindness, such as holding the door open for others, thanking their mail carrier or door attendant, and helping the elderly carry groceries. These small acts made a significant difference to their own happiness.

PEACE IS POSSIBLE

In the twenty-first century, increasing numbers of Canadian and U.S. citizens are investing their time and money in the pursuit of peace. This takes many forms—health programs; yoga; tai chi; meditation; participation in a church, mosque, or synagogue; and so on. Spiritual teachers from a wide variety of traditions are eager to assist in the pursuit of peace. Most of these teachers would agree that inner peace takes more than a one-step solution. Men and women experience peace when they exercise right, eat right, follow their chosen spiritual practices, and find ways to serve others. The first years of the new century have not been easy. Terrorism, wars, and natural disasters add to the stress of busy modern living. Yet many spiritual practitioners say they experience a frequent sense of inner peace. They experience what Thomas Kelly calls "Life from the Center."

LIVING PEACE

FURTHER READING

Bodian, Stephan. *Meditation for Dummies.* Foster City, Calif.: IDG Books, 1999.

De Mello, Anthony. *The Way to Love.* New York: Doubleday, 1991.

Fontana, David. *The Meditator's Handbook: A Comprehensive Guide to Eastern & Western Meditation Techniques.* Boston, Mass.: Element, 1992.

Foster, Richard. *Devotional Classics.* New York: HarperCollins, 1993.

Foster, Richard. *Celebration of Discipline: The Path to Spiritual Growth.* New York: HarperCollins, 1998.

Hanh, Thich Nhat. *Living Buddha, Living Christ.* New York: Riverhead Books, 1995.

Huggett, Joyce. *The Joy of Listening to God: Hearing the Many Ways God Speaks to Us.* Downers Grove, Ill.: InterVarsity Press, 1986.

Kelly, Thomas R. *A Testament of Devotion.* San Francisco, Calif.: HarperCollins, 1992.

Maguire, Jack. *Essential Buddhism: A Complete Guide to Beliefs and Practices.* New York: Pocket Books, 2001.

Nouwen, Henri J. M. *Desert Wisdom: Sayings from the Desert Fathers.* Maryknoll, N.Y.: Orbis, 2001.

Robinson, Jonathan. *The Complete Idiot's Guide to Awakening Your Spirituality.* Indianapolis, Ind.: Alpha, 2000.

Sittser, Jerry. *A Grace Disguised: How the Soul Grows Through Loss.* Grand Rapids, Mich.: Zondervan, 2005.

Smedes, Lewis. *Forgive and Forget: Healing the Hurts You Don't Deserve.* San Francisco, Calif.: Harper, 1996.

FOR MORE INFORMATION

Buddhanet
www.buddhanet.net/index.html

Christian Meditation
www.allaboutgod.com/
Christian-Meditation.htm

Joyful Heart Renewal Ministries
www.joyfulheart.com/

Meditation & Prayer @ Beliefnet
www.beliefnet.com/index/
index_201.html

Meditation Techniques &
Resources
healing.about.com/od/
meditation/

Meditation—Holistic Online.com
www.1stholistic.com/Meditation
/hol_meditation_healing.htm

The Tai Chi Netguide
www.soton.ac.uk/~maa1/chi/
home.htm

The Voice in the Stillness
www.frimmin.com/faith/
meditation.html

Yoga Basics
www.yogabasics.com/

Publisher's note:
The Web sites listed on this page were active at the time of publication.
The publisher is not responsible for Web sites that have changed their
addresses or discontinued operation since the date of publication. The
publisher will review and update the Web-site list upon each reprint.

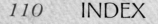

PICTURE CREDITS

The illustrations in RELIGION AND MODERN CULTURE are photo montages made by Dianne Hodack. They are a combination of her original mixed-media paintings and collages, the photography of Benjamin Stewart, various historical public-domain artwork, and other royalty-free photography collections.

AUTHORS: Kenneth and Marsha McIntosh are former teachers. They have two children, Jonathan, nineteen, and Eirené, sixteen. Marsha has a bachelor's of science degree in Bible and education, and Kenneth has a bachelor's degree in English education and a master's degree in theology. They live in Flagstaff, Arizona, with their children, a dog, and two cats. Kenneth frequently speaks on topics of religion and society. Kenneth and Marsha have been involved in a variety of political causes over the past two decades.

CONSULTANT: Dr. Marcus J. Borg is the Hundere Distinguished Professor of Religion and Culture in the Philosophy Department at Oregon State University. Dr. Borg is past president of the Anglican Association of Biblical Scholars. Internationally known as a biblical and Jesus scholar, the *New York Times* called him "a leading figure among this generation of Jesus scholars." He is the author of twelve books, which have been translated into eight languages. Among them are *The Heart of Christianity: Rediscovering a Life of Faith* (2003) and *Meeting Jesus Again for the First Time* (1994), the best-selling book by a contemporary Jesus scholar.

CONSULTANT: Dr. Robert K. Johnston is Professor of Theology and Culture at Fuller Theological Seminary in Pasadena, California, having served previously as Provost of North Park University and as a faculty member of Western Kentucky University. The author or editor of thirteen books and twenty-five book chapters (including *The Christian at Play*, 1983; *The Variety of American Evangelicalism*, 1991; *Reel Spirituality: Theology and Film in Dialogue*, 2000; *Life Is Not Work/Work Is Not Life: Simple Reminders for Finding Balance in a 24/7 World*, 2000; *Finding God in the Movies: 33 Films of Reel Faith*, 2004; and *Useless Beauty: Ecclesiastes Through the Lens of Contemporary Film*, 2004), Johnston is the immediate past president of the American Theological Society, an ordained Protestant minister, and an avid bodysurfer.